For my mum

Hello
Mr Scarecrow

written and illustrated by
Rob Lewis

A Sunburst Book

Farrar Straus Giroux

In January,
the farmer made Mr Scarecrow with –

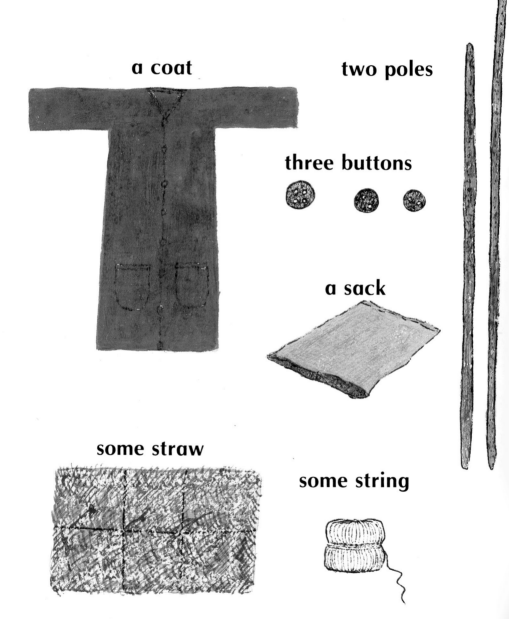

a coat

two poles

three buttons

a sack

some straw

some string

Hello Mr Scarecrow.

In February,
Mr Scarecrow was put out in the field.

**In March,
the sparrows came to steal straw
for their nests.**

In April,
the moles popped up
to sniff the warm spring air.

In May,
the slugs and snails came to say hello.

In June, some cows got loose

and nearly knocked Mr Scarecrow down.

In July,
the rabbits played in the evening sun.

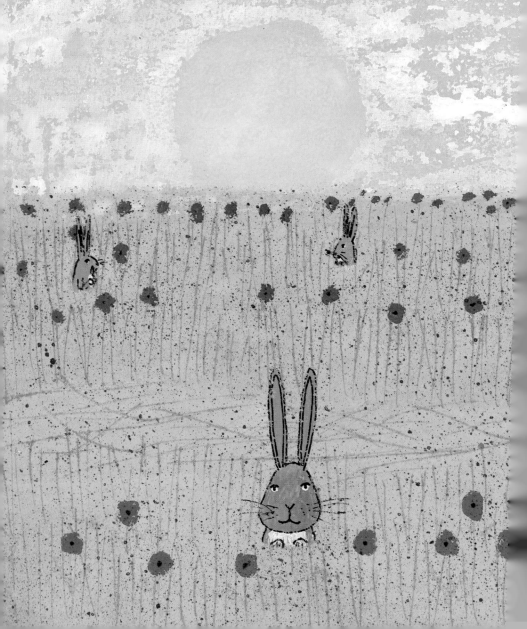

In August,
the harvest mice made their nests.

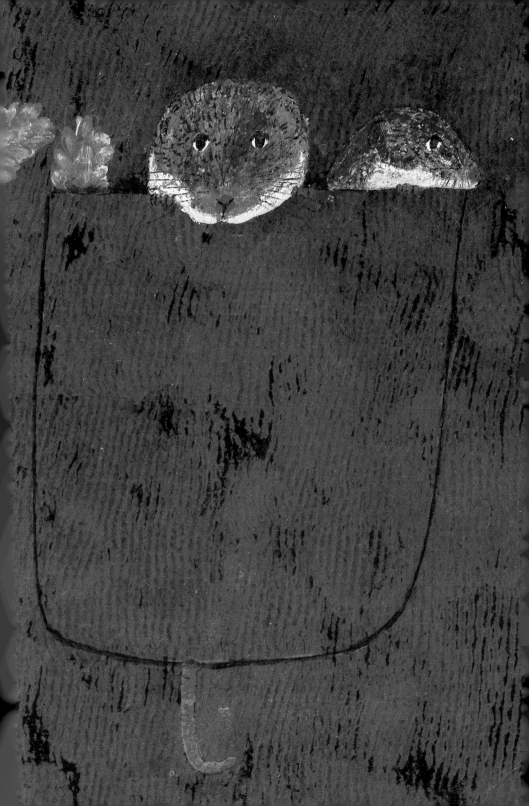

In September, the corn was harvested.
Mr Scarecrow watched.

In October,
the foxes came out to hunt by moonlight.

In November,
the badgers plodded home
to their winter beds.

In December, the crows came closer.
They weren't scared of Mr Scarecrow.

In January,
the children came to play.

Goodbye Mr Scarecrow.

Copyright © 1987 by Rob Lewis
All rights reserved
First published in Great Britain in 1987
by Macdonald & Co (Publishers) Ltd
First American edition, 1987
Library of Congress catalog card number: 86-46443
Printed and bound in Spain
Sunburst edition, 1988